SHACK and BACK

Michael Crowley

Illustrated by Abby Carter

Little, Brown and Company

Boston   Toronto   London

A portion of the royalties earned by the author
of this book is being donated to
Literacy Volunteers of America, Inc.

Text copyright © 1993 by Michael Crowley
Illustrations copyright © 1993 by Abby Carter

First Edition

Library of Congress Cataloging-in-Publication Data

Crowley, Michael.
    Shack and back / Michael Crowley ; illustrated by Abby Carter. —
1st ed.
    p.   cm.
    Summary: Crater insults T-Ball and causes her to quit the Spurwink
Gang, just when they need her riding talent to win a bike race.
    ISBN 0-316-16231-0
    [1. Gangs — Fiction.   2. Bicycle racing — Fiction.]   I. Carter,
Abby, ill.   II. Title.
PZ7.C8876Sh   1993
[E] — dc20   91-44473

10 9 8 7 6 5 4 3 2 1
SC

Published simultaneously in Canada
by Little, Brown & Company (Canada) Limited
Printed in Hong Kong

For Kathryn, Maggie, and Michael
— M. C.

For Granny
— A. C.

Of all the dumb things Tim "Crater" Creighton ever said, and there were plenty, the dumbest of all was when he said, "Cooking is for sissy-girls."

Crater wanted to go digging for clams down at Kettle Cove.
Denise Dipetro wanted to go to her house and make mini-pizzas.
And before the rest of the Spurwink Gang could decide, Crater
went and said it.

"What!?" said T-Ball Knowles, her face tightening.

"Sissy-girls?!" said Bonnie Bouchard.

"What a jerk!" said her twin sister, Leslie.

"Oughtta sissy you one!" said Denise Dipetro, making a fist.

"Uh-oh," said Jimmy Raymond, and the gang split up right then and there. Boys one way, girls the other.

"Crater," Jimmy Ray said later, "this is a bad situation, with the girls and all."

"Ah, buncha tea bags," Crater said. "Who wants girls in a gang anyway? Mostly they're useless. I say it's time to ditch 'em — for good. Huh, Leonard, you with me?"

Leonard said, "Naw, man. Then it's just us three. That's kind of a puny gang."

"Well, fine!" Crater shouted. "Why don't we just put on dresses and sit around giggling?!"

"C'mon, Crater," Jimmy Ray said. "The girls have always been part of the gang."

"Yeah, well" — Crater picked up his clam bucket — "maybe it's time for a change."

Over at Denise's, the girls were still mad.

"What is it with those guys?" Denise said. "Since when are they so special?"

"Yeah, and what's the big deal about clamming?" Bonnie said. "We always dig more than they do anyway."

"Buncha crab-heads," T-Ball said. "Maybe we ought to just kick them out of the Spurwink Gang."

"Can we *do* that?" Leslie asked.

T-Ball took a big bite of pizza. "Why not?"

As the tide moved back into Kettle Cove, the boys headed up to their bikes.

"Let's go over to my house," Jimmy Ray said. "I'll ask my mom to steam these clams up for lunch, and then —" He stopped suddenly, looking up the path.

"Aw, this is bad," Leonard whispered. "This is very bad."

For there, standing right in their way, were Ernest McVane
and the Broad Cove Bullies.

"Aaaaay, Winkies!" Ernest shouted. "Where ya been hidin'?
Haven't seen ya 'round lately."

"We've been around," Jimmy Ray said.

"Hey, is that for us?" Ernest knocked over Leonard's clam bucket.

"Naw, man." Leonard scrambled to pick up the clams. "Don't do that."

"Gee, I'm *so* sorry," Ernest sneered. "Hey, you guys got some nice wheels here — whoops!" He pushed Crater's bike over. "Oh, gee, it slipped."

"Knock it off!" Crater said.

"Yeah? Or what?" Ernest said. "You'll sic the *girls* on us?" The other Bullies started laughing. "Hey, where are they, anyway? Shouldn't you all be playing patty cake or something?"

"Don't *have* any girls in the Spurwink Gang," Crater blurted out.

"What? No girls? Since when?"

"Since we don't *need* 'em," Crater said.

"Yeah, I can see you guys are pretty tough," Ernest said, and the Bullies chuckled some more. "In fact, I'll bet if we said, 'How about a bike race — your gang's fastest rider against ours — down to the Lobster Shack and back,' I bet you'd say yes."

No one said anything.

"And if we said, 'Losers wash winners' bikes,' you'd say, 'You're on.'"

No one said anything.

"What? We didn't quite hear that."

Crater's face was red as a beet. "You're on," he said.

"Hey, OK!" Ernest said. "We'll get our bikes. See you back here in one hour." And the Bullies went off toward Broad Cove, laughing and slapping each other on the back.

"Oh, great," Jimmy Ray said. "Might as well just get some sponges. We'll be washing bikes all afternoon."

"Hey, we can beat these guys," Crater said. "Can't we?"

"Naw, man," said Leonard. "None of us can."

"There is *one* person who could," Jimmy Ray said. " 'Course she's not in the gang anymore, right, Crater?"

"Oh, no," Crater said, "not T-Ball. We'll just get laughed at."

"What for?" Leonard said.

"What for?!" Crater yelled. "What for?! Well . . . she's a girl!"

Leonard and Jimmy Ray just looked at him.

"Hey, you guys know what I mean," Crater said. "Don't you?"

"No," Leonard said.

"Me either," said Jimmy Ray. "All I know is T-Ball's a lot faster than any of us."

"But it's embarrassing!" Crater said.

"Yeah?" Leonard said. "What if she won?"

Crater's eyes widened. He hadn't thought of that.

"She's our only chance," Jimmy Ray said.

The girls were playing on the rope swing at Denise's when
the boys pulled up.

"Hey, guess what?" Jimmy Ray yelled to the girls.

They ignored him.

"Big bike race this afternoon."

They kept swinging.

"Starts at Kettle Cove in one hour. Our fastest rider against
the Bullies' fastest. Shack and back. Loser gang has to wash the
winner's bikes. Whattya think?"

T-Ball looked up. A big grin worked its way across her face. "Who's riding for you?" she said.

"You mean who's riding for *us*, don't you?" Jimmy Ray said.

T-Ball just smiled and looked at Crater.

"C'mon, T-Ball." Jimmy Ray was pleading now. "Everybody knows you're the fastest rider in the Spurwink Gang. You gotta do this."

"Gee, I'd like to," T-Ball said. "But we've just got too much 'sissy-girl' stuff to do, don't we, girls?"

The girls all smirked. "Oh, yes."

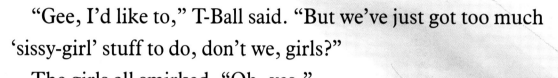

"Wait," Jimmy Ray said, "Crater has something he wants
to say. . . . Crater?"

"Imfry," Crater said, staring at his feet.

"What?" said the girls.

"I'M SORRY," Crater yelled, "OK? Are you happy now?
I'M SORRY I'M SORRY I'M SORRY!!!"

"Boy oh boy," T-Ball said, "you better relax. Save some
energy for all those bikes you're gonna have to wash."

Crater made a kind of strangled noise and rode off.

Jimmy Ray went up to T-Ball and said quietly, "This could
be the end of the Spurwink Gang, you know."

"It doesn't look good, does it?" T-Ball said.

As race time approached, the Spurwink boys had all but
given up.

"Aaaaay, Winkies!" Here came Ernest. "What's the matter?
You look like you all lost a friend."

"A bunch of them," Jimmy Ray said to himself.

"Get ready to scrub-a-dub," Ernest said. "One minute
till race time . . . thirty seconds. . . . Where's your
rider, Winkies?"

Suddenly there came a shout: "Right here, Ernest!" It
was T-Ball! With the rest of the girls riding right behind her.

"Yes!" cried Jimmy Ray.

"Yee-how!" Crater yelled, and the whole gang started chanting, "T-BALL, T-BALL, T-BALL!"

"Wait a minute," Ernest said, pointing at T-Ball. "You said no girls. She can't be in on this."

"Hey, Ernest," T-Ball said, "you wanna race, or you wanna be a . . . sissy-boy?"

Ernest tightened up his chin strap. "Let's go."

T-Ball waxed him, of course, and the Spurwink Gang sat around all afternoon eating steamed clams and watching the Bullies wash bikes.

"I've been thinking," T-Ball said after a while. "It might be fun to have a . . . tea party tomorrow. Dress up a little, use our manners, pretend we're important guests. What do you say?"

Everyone looked at Crater.

Through clenched teeth he said, "It sounds like . . . fun."

T-Ball winked, and the whole Spurwink Gang laughed
together.